THE AMERICAN GIRLS

1764 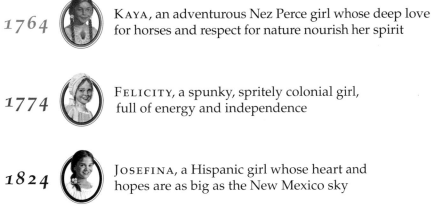 KAYA, an adventurous Nez Perce girl whose deep love for horses and respect for nature nourish her spirit

1774 FELICITY, a spunky, spritely colonial girl, full of energy and independence

1824 JOSEFINA, a Hispanic girl whose heart and hopes are as big as the New Mexico sky

1854 KIRSTEN, a pioneer girl of strength and spirit who settles on the frontier

1864 ADDY, a courageous girl determined to be free in the midst of the Civil War

1904 SAMANTHA, a bright Victorian beauty, an orphan raised by her wealthy grandmother

1934 KIT, a clever, resourceful girl facing the Great Depression with spirit and determination

1944 MOLLY, who schemes and dreams on the home front during World War Two

1974 JULIE, a fun-loving girl from San Francisco who faces big changes—and creates a few of her own

1932
REALLY TRULY
Ruthie

BY VALERIE TRIPP

ILLUSTRATIONS WALTER RANE

VIGNETTES SUSAN MCALILEY

★ American Girl®

Questions or comments? Call 1-800-845-0005, visit our Web site at
americangirl.com, or write to Customer Service, American Girl,
8400 Fairway Place, Middleton, WI 53562.

Printed in China
08 09 10 11 12 13 14 LEO 10 9 8 7 6 5 4

PICTURE CREDITS
The following individuals and organizations have generously given
permission to reprint images contained in "Looking Back":
p. 61—© Christie's Images/Corbis; p. 62—© Bettmann/Corbis;
p. 63—© Minnesota Historical Society/Corbis (car and men);
p. 64—© David J. and Janice L. Frent Collection/Corbis (CCC pennant);
© Bettmann/Corbis (WPA poster); FDR Library (Eleanor Roosevelt);
p. 65—FDR Library (My Day column); © Alan Jakubek/Corbis (apples);
p. 66—Western Reserve Historical Society, Cleveland, OH (car and women);
from *When the Banks Closed, Our Hearts Opened* (Reminisce Books);
p. 67—from *When the Banks Closed, Our Hearts Opened*

Cataloging-in-Publication Data available from the Library of Congress.

TO ROBERT SCHUYLER HEUER,
WITH LOVE

TABLE OF CONTENTS

RUTHIE'S FRIENDS

CHAPTER ONE
APPLES AND KINDNESS 1

CHAPTER TWO
GOOFY RUTHIE 19

CHAPTER THREE
EAST OF THE SUN
AND WEST OF THE MOON 33

CHAPTER FOUR
WISHES COME TRUE 47

LOOKING BACK 61

A SNEAK PEEK AT *MEET KIT* 69

RUTHIE'S FRIENDS

RUTHIE
A nine-year-old girl who is a loyal, understanding, and generous friend

KIT
Ruthie's best friend, who is clever and resourceful in helping her family cope with the dark days of the Depression

CHARLIE
Kit's affectionate and supportive older brother

AUNT MILLIE
The lively and loving woman who raised Kit's dad

MRS. KITTREDGE
*Kit's mother, who takes
care of her family and
their home with strength
and determination*

MR. KITTREDGE
*Kit's father, a businessman
facing the problems of the
Great Depression*

MRS. HOWARD
*Mrs. Kittredge's garden
club friend, who is a guest
in the Kittredge home*

**STIRLING
HOWARD**
*Mrs. Howard's son, whose
delicate health hides
surprising strengths*

CHAPTER
ONE

APPLES AND KINDNESS

Once upon a time! Ruthie thought happily as she hurried along the icy sidewalk. *That's how all wonderful adventures begin.* And Ruthie was sure, this sparkling cold morning, that she was at the beginning of a wonderful adventure. Most people would probably say that Christmas or their birthday was their favorite day, but not Ruthie Smithens. For Ruthie, today—December twenty-sixth, the day after Christmas—was the best day of the year because *this* was when Ruthie and her best friend, Kit Kittredge, had a special day with their mothers. It was their tradition to go on an outing together in downtown Cincinnati. Ruthie could not wait for their special day to begin. She walked toward Kit's house as fast as she could, which wasn't very fast because she was carrying a crate with apples in it.

When Ruthie got to Kit's house, she balanced the crate on one hip and knocked on the door with her free hand. The apples were heavy, so she was glad when the door was flung open almost immediately by Kit.

"Hi, Ruthie!" said Kit with a huge smile. She held the door while Ruthie brought the apple crate inside. "Come on in. You're just in time!" Then Kit called over Ruthie's shoulder, "Hey, everybody! Ruthie's here!"

A cheerful chorus of voices called out from the dining room, "Hi, Ruthie!" Ever since Mr. Kittredge lost his job because of the Depression, the Kittredges had earned money by renting rooms in their house to boarders, so there was always a crowd at the breakfast table.

"Just in time for what?" Ruthie asked Kit eagerly, puffing a little as they lowered the crate of apples to the floor.

"To say good-bye," said Kit. "Dad's got a job driving two of our friends, Mr. and Mrs. Bell, to

"Hey, everybody! Ruthie's here!" called Kit.

Florida. Mrs. Bell doesn't know how to drive and Mr. Bell's eyesight isn't very good, so they asked Dad to drive them. They're going to spend the winter in Florida with their grandson, and then, in the spring, they'll come back and move in here. They're just about to leave. Come on."

Ruthie was an only child. She and her parents, who were the kindest people in the world, lived in a big beautiful house that was tidy, calm, and quiet. In fact, it was entirely *too* tidy, calm, and quiet, in Ruthie's opinion. That's why Ruthie loved Kit's house; there was always *something* going on.

Chaos and commotion were going on right now. Mr. Kittredge had his hat jammed on the back of his head, his coat half on, and a napkin tucked in his collar. He and Kit's brother, Charlie, and one of the boarders, Mr. Peck, were at the table talking all at the same time as they studied a big map that was spread out on top of coffee cups and juice glasses. Miss Hart and Miss Finney, two nurses who were boarders, were helping Mrs. Kittredge stack and clear the breakfast dishes.

Mrs. Howard, a fussbudgety boarder, was earnestly trying to convince Mrs. Bell to borrow her son Stirling's hot water bottle, and Mrs. Bell was just as earnestly saying, "No, no thank you, really, no thank you." Mr. Bell, who for some reason had both his own and Mrs. Bell's hats on his head, was shaking hands and saying good-bye to everyone over and over again. He shook hands with Ruthie twice before Mrs. Kittredge herded the whole crowd outside and the Bells and Mr. Kittredge climbed into the overloaded car. Kit, Ruthie, Stirling, and Charlie ran down the driveway following the car, waving and calling out good-byes that were lost in the honks of the car horn. Just when the car reached the street, it stopped short. Mr. Kittredge jumped out, ran back, and kissed Mrs. Kittredge good-bye while everyone laughed and hooted and cheered.

"Well!" said Mrs. Kittredge, smoothing her hair after the car finally disappeared. "I guess they're well and truly on their way at last."

"How long will your dad be gone?" Ruthie asked Kit as they walked inside toward the kitchen.

"Eight days," said Kit. "Four days down to Florida in the Bells' car and four days driving someone else's car back up."

Ruthie counted on her fingers. "So he'll be back on January second, right?" she asked.

"Yes," said Kit. "Definitely."

The two girls exchanged a quick, uncomfortable glance. Neither one wanted to say so, but they both knew that Mr. Kittredge *had* to be back by January second and with payment for his driving jobs in hand. The Kittredges were in a desperate situation. Even though they worked very hard running their boarding house, they owed the bank so much money that the bank was going to take their house away from them if they did not pay some of the money back. If Kit's family were to lose their house, then they'd lose their boarders, too—and the boarders were their main source of income. Ruthie's father, Mr. Smithens, worked for the bank. It had been his sad job before Christmas to tell the Kittredges that he had held off the bank as long as he could and that the Kittredges were going to be evicted—thrown out of their house—after the holidays if they did not pay the bank. Ruthie didn't know how much Mr. Kittredge was going to be paid for his two driving jobs, but she sure hoped it was enough to stop the bank from taking the house.

"Hey, Kit," said Ruthie, tactfully changing to a nicer subject. "You remember what day it is today, don't you?"

"Of course I do!" said Kit, hopping happily. "It's *our* day. The best day of the year!" She took Ruthie's hand and pulled her toward the kitchen. "Come on. Let's ask my mother how soon she'll be ready to go."

It was warm in the kitchen and noisy with the clatter of dishes being washed by Mrs. Kittredge and Mrs. Howard. Charlie and Stirling were lifting the crate of apples onto the kitchen table just as Kit and Ruthie walked in.

"I bet you brought these apples, Ruthie," said Stirling in his surprisingly low, husky voice.

"Right," said Charlie. He liked to tease Ruthie about her interest in fairy tales. "I suppose you waved your magic wand and made them appear."

"Not quite," said Ruthie. "I lugged them here. My mother asked me to. Someone gave us tons of apples for Christmas, and Mother was hoping you could use some so that they won't go to waste."

"Nothing's wasted around here," said Charlie, "especially nothing to eat. Stirling and I see to that."

He took an apple out of the crate for himself and tossed another to Stirling.

"Thank you, Ruthie," said Mrs. Kittredge, "and please thank your mother for us, too."

"You're welcome," said Ruthie. She was secretly relieved that the apples had been accepted without a fuss. Ruthie and her mother were in cahoots; they had a conspiracy of kindness going on in which they tried to find ways to help the Kittredges whenever they could. But Ruthie had learned the hard way that generosity was tricky. She had to be very careful and respectful about giving things to Kit and her family. Take their special day, for example. Ruthie and Kit had had a serious fight just before Christmas, when Ruthie had told Kit that she and her mother would treat Kit and her mother to the ballet and lunch in a restaurant. Kit's prickly pride had been so offended that they wouldn't be having their special day today at *all* if both girls hadn't compromised.

Kit spoke up. "Mother," she said, "you and I can thank Mrs. Smithens ourselves. Today's our special day together. Remember?"

An anxious look tightened Mrs. Kittredge's face.

"Oh, dear," she sighed. "I just don't know if I . . ."
She glanced toward the laundry room, where a
huge basket piled mountain-high with sheets and
tablecloths sat on the ironing board, and the drying
rack was draped with napkins and dish towels.
"There's all the Christmas linen to wash and iron.
And I want to give our room a thorough cleaning
before your father comes back. I really should make
applesauce now that we have all these apples, and
I promised Uncle Hendrick that I would spend
the night at his house because he's feeling poorly
again."

Just when Ruthie and Kit's hopes were faltering,
help came from a most unexpected person. "My
land!" fussed Mrs. Howard, her usually fluttery
voice firm for once. "You mustn't even consider
missing your special day with the girls, Margaret.
I won't hear of it. Charlie, Stirling, and I will handle
the chores, and gladly. Won't we, boys?"

Charlie grabbed a giant box of Sudso and put
the colander upside down on his head like a helmet.
He saluted Mrs. Howard and said, "Yes, sir!"

"It will be my Christmas present to you," Stirling
said to Mrs. Kittredge quietly.

"There! That's settled," said Mrs. Howard, pink-cheeked and pleased with her new bossy self. She waved Mrs. Kittredge and the girls out of the kitchen with the soapy spoon she was washing. "Off you go now."

It was as if Mrs. Howard's soapy spoon really were the magic wand Charlie had teased Ruthie about, because, *abracadabra,* quick as a wink, Ruthie and Kit found themselves running and sliding on the slick sidewalk ahead of Mrs. Kittredge on their way to the Smithenses' house. When Mrs. Smithens met them at the door, Ruthie threw her arms around her mother and said exuberantly, "I brought Kit and her mother with me. They're ready to go."

Mrs. Smithens widened her hug to include Kit. She smiled at Mrs. Kittredge. "How lovely to see you, Margaret," she said. "Are you prepared to spend the day with these two wild creatures?"

Mrs. Kittredge laughed, and Ruthie was delighted to see no trace of any anxious look on her face. "Well, Lily," Mrs. Kittredge said to Mrs. Smithens, "I'm game if you are."

Downtown Cincinnati, still decked out in its Christmas wreaths and bows, looked like an enchanted

Mrs. Howard waved them out of the kitchen with the soapy spoon she was washing. "Off you go now," she said.

city. A mischievous breeze made the shiny silver, gold, red, and green spangles on the streetlight poles bob and catch the sunshine so that light and color sparkled everywhere. Mrs. Smithens parked the car, and she and Mrs. Kittredge strolled slowly along behind Kit and Ruthie, who swooped swiftly from store window to store window, exclaiming and pointing out the wonders within to one another.

"Oh, look!" said Kit, pointing to a snowy mountain scene inside one window. A fat snowman made of glitter sat in an old-fashioned horse-drawn sleigh waving his stick arms, which actually moved. The sleigh was silver and white, the horses were silver and white, and giant silver and white snowflakes hung from fine threads all around the sleigh and twinkled in the sunlight.

"It reminds me of the silver forest the twelve dancing princesses sneak through on their way to the ball," said Ruthie.

Kit was sometimes impatient with Ruthie and her interest in fairy-tale princesses, but today she smiled indulgently. "Don't you wish you could be in that sleigh, flying down that mountain?" Kit asked.

"Yes," said Ruthie fervently, "I do. It's been a wish of mine all my life to ride in a sleigh like that."

Ruthie and Kit had agreed that all of the activities they did on their special day had to be free. That was their compromise. So after window-shopping, the girls and their mothers went to Union Station, where a brass band was playing, and then to the park to watch the ice-skaters. The skating looked like so much fun that Kit and Ruthie slid around the ice in their shoes. Ruthie, who loved to make Kit laugh, pretended to be a rather clumsy ballerina who pirouetted and then, *plonk!*, plopped down on the ice. After that the girls were starving, so they sat in the cozy car with their mothers and had a picnic. Mrs. Smithens had brought thick sandwiches and thermoses of coffee for the grown-ups and hot chocolate for the girls. Mrs. Kittredge had brought a basket that had dessert in it: chocolate chip cookies wrapped in red bandannas. After lunch, the girls and their mothers walked to the beautiful fountain in the center of the city. Kit and Ruthie

posed like the statues in the fountain and made up
stories about them while Mrs. Kittredge and Mrs.
Smithens stood arm in arm, watching the girls and
sometimes talking, bending their heads together like
graceful birds.

It was very cold and windy, and after a while
the girls were lightly misted with spray blown
from melted ice on the fountain, so they were glad
to climb into the car again. Mrs. Smithens drove
slowly along streets lined with houses, and the
girls chose the ones they thought had the best
decorations. As the winter afternoon sky turned
pink and purple, the girls could see people's
Christmas trees light up inside their windows,
suddenly, as if by magic.

Ruthie was completely happy. *If I were in a fairy
tale and I had three wishes,* Ruthie thought, *I'd use them
ALL to wish that we could always be the way we are right
now, with everyone relaxed and not thinking about the
terrible old Depression or awful things like being evicted.
That truly would be living happily ever after.*

But even special days have to end, and so
Mrs. Smithens dropped Kit and her mother at their
Uncle Hendrick's house. Ruthie was glad to see

that in the flurry of good-byes and thank-yous, her mother managed to put all the leftovers from their picnic into Mrs. Kittredge's basket without the Kittredges noticing. After the Kittredges left, Ruthie sat in the front seat with her mother and snuggled up to her. Mrs. Smithens's coat smelled like a delicious combination of perfume and cold air. "Thank you, Mom," said Ruthie. "That was the best special day we've ever had."

"Thank *you*, dear," said Mrs. Smithens. "Mrs. Kittredge and I enjoy our outing as much as you and Kit do."

Ruthie sighed. "Oh, I *wish* there was more we could do to help Kit's family," she said. "Can't we give them some money?"

"I offered once, a while ago," said Mrs. Smithens. "And I know that your father has offered several times. But Mr. and Mrs. Kittredge said no very, very firmly. It would be rude to ask again. I'm afraid all we can give is kindness."

"And things like apples," added Ruthie.

"Apples and kindness," said Mrs. Smithens. "It sounds crazy, but I'm afraid that's all that makes sense at a time like this." She smiled at Ruthie. "I know what," she said. "Let's go to the bank and see if we can give your father a ride home. What do you say?"

"Yes!" said Ruthie.

Everyone who worked at the bank smiled and nodded and said hello as Ruthie and her mother went past on their way to Mr. Smithens's office. Ruthie saw that her dad was reading some papers on his desk and frowning. But when he looked up and saw Ruthie and her mother, he pulled off his glasses and smiled. "What a nice surprise!" he said. "How are my two best girls?"

"We're fine!" said Ruthie. She hugged her father, and then she jumped into his desk chair, which she loved because it tilted back and spun around.

"We're here to drive you home," said Mrs. Smithens.

Ruthie was spinning, so she did not see her father's face, but she could tell from his voice that he'd lost his smile. "I'd love that, darling," he was saying to Ruthie's mother, drawing her toward the window. "But I'm afraid I have a few more hours of work to do."

Ruthie continued to spin as her parents spoke softly over by the

window. She spun so fast that pretty soon she began
to feel dizzy and had to grab the desk to stop. By
mistake, she knocked some folders off the desk.
As she gathered them up, her eye caught the name
KITTREDGE written in angry black letters on a
note clipped to the folder. Ruthie didn't mean to
snoop—she really didn't! But she could not help
staring at the note. As she read it she felt dizzy again,
this time dizzy with dismay. Because the note made
it absolutely clear: the Kittredges were going to be
evicted from their house. And not on January second,
as they had all thought, but on December twenty-
eighth. The Kittredges and Mr. Smithens must have
misunderstood what the bank meant by "after the
holidays."

Ruthie could hardly breathe. December twenty-
eighth was the day after tomorrow! Mr. Kittredge
would not be back from Florida with the money by
then. Oh, what on earth could the Kittredges do?
What could *anyone* do to help them? Ruthie knew
that there was no use in talking to her parents about
it. Kind as they were, there was nothing they could
do this time. The Kittredges wouldn't accept money
from them, and her father couldn't delay the bank

17

anymore from proceeding with the eviction.

With all her heart, Ruthie wished that she could save Kit and her family. But she knew that apples and kindness weren't going to be enough at this point. The Kittredges needed money and they needed it *fast*.

CHAPTER TWO

GOOFY RUTHIE

 Ruthie was quiet in the car on the way home. "Tired, sweetheart?" her mother asked.

"A little," said Ruthie. "But may I stop off at Kit's house and walk home afterwards? I need to talk to Kit for a minute. She should be home from her Uncle Hendrick's by now."

"All right, dear, but don't stay long," said her mother. "You know that Kit has chores to do, and you've both had a long day."

"Thanks, Mom," said Ruthie. She hopped out of the car and ran to Kit's door.

This time it was Charlie who opened the door when Ruthie knocked. "Hey!" he teased. "Ruthie!

Long time no see."

Ruthie blushed. Was Charlie hinting that she was
a pest? Well, she could not worry about that right
now. She had to see Kit right away. "Are Kit and
your mother back from your Uncle Hendrick's?"
she asked.

"Mother's staying at Uncle Hendrick's tonight
and tomorrow," said Charlie. "But Kit's back. She's
in the kitchen. Gosh, Ruthie, what's your hurry?
Didn't you two spend the day together?"

But Ruthie couldn't stop to answer.
She ran full tilt to the kitchen. Luckily,
Kit was alone, peeling apples. She
looked surprised to see Ruthie.

Ruthie held up her hand to stop Kit from
talking. "Kit," she said urgently, "I saw a paper
at the bank. You—your family—you're going to be
evicted December twenty-eighth. That's the day after
tomorrow."

"But," gasped Kit, "they said *after* the holidays!"

"I guess the bank meant after the *Christmas*
holiday, not the New Year's holiday," said Ruthie.
"Now listen, Kit, don't get mad at me. But my
grandparents gave me ten dollars for Christmas

20

and please, you've got to take it and—"

"No," Kit interrupted, shaking her head. "Thanks, but ten dollars won't solve our problem. We owe more than two hundred dollars." Tiredly, Kit untied her apron. "I'll have to go to Uncle Hendrick's and tell Mother the bad news about December twenty-eighth," she said.

"It will be hard," said Ruthie. "But your Uncle Hendrick is rich. Your mother can ask *him* for the money."

"She already did," said Kit, slowly and miserably, "and he already said no." Suddenly Kit slumped into a chair and put her head in her hands. Ruthie had never seen her friend look so defeated. She sat down, too, and listened as Kit poured out all her sorrow.

"Mother will be so upset," Kit said. "Uncle Hendrick will say 'I told you so.' He'll gloat and be glad. Uncle Hendrick wants us to lose our house and have to move into his gloomy old house with him and be servants for him. We'll have to, if we do lose the house. Because then we'll lose the boarders, too, and they're the only hope we have. Oh, being evicted would be so awful, so *humiliating*."

Ruthie knew exactly what Kit meant. She and
Kit had both seen the sad, disgraceful sight of a
family's furniture and household goods—books,
pots and pans, toys, and clothes—dumped in a
jumble on the sidewalk for all to see because the
family had been evicted from their house. Ruthie
could not bear the thought of such a horrible thing
happening to Kit and her family. There had to be
some way to get the money to prevent it.

Ruthie spoke gently. "What about your Aunt
Millie?" she asked. "She'd lend you the money,
wouldn't she?"

Kit nodded.

"I know what," said Ruthie. "Let's go to my

house and call Aunt Millie right now."
The Kittredges didn't have a phone
anymore because they couldn't afford it,
so they used the Smithenses' phone when
they needed to make a call. "If Aunt
Millie came here on the train tomorrow

telephone   and brought the money, you'd have it in
plenty of time. Tomorrow's only the twenty-seventh
of December."

"Aunt Millie doesn't have a phone," said Kit.

"There's only one phone in the whole county and it's miles away from her cabin. A letter wouldn't get to her in time. So I guess the only solution would be for Mother to go see Aunt Millie and bring the money back. Poor Mother! Where she'd even get the train fare, I don't know."

Ruthie's heart beat hard. She had an idea. "What if *you and I* go get the money?" she said.

Kit made a face and shook her head. "Don't be silly, Ruthie," she said.

"I'm not being silly," said Ruthie. "I have never been more serious in my life. Listen to this plan: Tomorrow, you and I use my ten dollars and buy train tickets. We go to Aunt Millie's, get the money, and bring it back. Then I give it to my father, he puts it in the bank on December twenty-eighth, and the whole problem is solved without any worry or sha—" Ruthie stopped.

"Or shame," Kit finished for her.

Ruthie nodded.

"That's a crazy plan," said Kit.

Ruthie remembered what her mother had said about apples and kindness. "Crazy makes sense at a time like this," Ruthie said. "We've got to at least try, Kit. Your mother's going to be at Uncle Hendrick's all day tomorrow, and my mother will be volunteering at the soup kitchen until late. With any luck, we'll be back with the money before anyone knows we're gone."

"I'd have to work it out with Charlie to do my afternoon chores for me," Kit said slowly. "I guess I could tell Mrs. Howard that I'm spending the day with you, and you could tell your mother that you're spending the day with me, which will be true."

"Does that mean you'll do it?" Ruthie asked.

"I guess it does," said Kit, as if she could hardly believe it herself.

"Good," said Ruthie quickly. She stood up. "I'll go to Union Station early tomorrow morning to buy the tickets while you do your morning chores. Then I'll meet you at the station at eight-thirty. Our train leaves at eight-forty-five. I know because it's the same train I take when I go to horseback-riding lessons. Don't be late." Then she left before Kit could change her mind.

train schedule

❧

24

Where is Kit? Ruthie wondered the next morning. She looked at her wristwatch. *It's already after eight-thirty.* Ruthie searched the bustling crowd at Union Station, eager to see her friend's familiar face. But when she did see a familiar face, Ruthie's heart sank. *Oh, no!* she thought. It was Charlie.

Union Station

Quickly, Ruthie shrank into the corner of the wooden bench she was sitting on. She tried to hide her face behind her pocketbook, hoping that Charlie would not see her. A second later, Ruthie felt a tug on the bow on top of her hat. She saw two big feet planted in front of her. Ruthie looked up with only her eyes, saying nothing.

"Okay, goofy Ruthie," said Charlie. "The jig is up. I'm here to take you home."

Ruthie didn't move.

"Come on, Ruthie," said Charlie. "Kit told me all about the crazy plan, and I called the whole thing off. So let's go home."

Ruthie sat stubbornly, as if she were glued to the bench.

Charlie sighed and sat down next to her. "Listen,

Ruthie," he said patiently. "It's nice of you to want to help, but you can't. I know you think that you're setting off on a quest like the hero in a fairy tale, some story that begins with 'once upon a time' and ends 'happily ever after'. But you're not. This is real life, not one of your fairy tales, and you're just a kid."

Ruthie frowned. She *had* sort of thought that the trip would be like an adventure in a story, but she did not want to admit that to Charlie. "You can't talk me out of this," she said. "So don't bother trying. I'm going to Aunt Millie's."

"That's ridiculous," said Charlie. "You've never been to Mountain Hollow or Aunt Millie's cabin. You've never even met Aunt Millie. How will you find her?"

"People will help me," said Ruthie. "I'm going, and that's final."

"Ruthie," Charlie began, "you are *not*—"

"I already bought the tickets," Ruthie cut in. "Round trip."

"What?" Charlie asked. He gave an exasperated sigh. Then he slapped his legs and stood up. "Well," he said, towering over Ruthie, "if you're going to Mountain Hollow, then I'm going, too. That's the deal."

Ruthie looked down at her lap so that Charlie could not see her expression. She knew perfectly well that just about everybody at Kit's house had the same opinion of her that Charlie did. They all thought that she was goofy Ruthie, more at home in the imaginary world of fairy-tale princesses than the real world of the Depression. She was funny and nice, but *not* practical or capable. Even Stirling and Kit, her very best friends, believed that Ruthie didn't really, truly know how damaging and terrible the Depression was because her father had not lost his job. They underestimated Ruthie's compassion and how deeply she felt their sorrows and losses as her own. Most of the time, it was okay with Ruthie not to be taken too seriously. She even deliberately pretended to be daffy and flighty sometimes, just to cheer everyone up and make them relax and laugh. But right now, Ruthie was tired of being dismissed.

Ruthie stood up and looked Charlie straight in the eye. *All right, let him come along,* she said to herself. *I'll show him. In fact, I'll show them all. I'll get the money no matter what happens. And then, instead of giving the money to my father, I will give it to Mrs. Kittredge, right in front of everybody. And when I do, no one will think I'm goofy Ruthie ever again.*

Aloud Ruthie said, "All right. It's a deal." She held her hand out and Charlie shook it. "Our train is boarding now." Ruthie picked up the basket of sandwiches and apples she had brought, as all good adventurers do. "Follow me."

Charlie followed Ruthie through the crowded station, down the platform, and onto the train. When they were settled in their seats, Charlie asked, "How'd you know how to buy the tickets, and which train we needed to take, and how to read the schedule and all?"

"Oh," said Ruthie breezily, "I take this eight-forty-five train a lot. Almost every Saturday, in fact. I take horseback-riding lessons just across the river in Fort Thomas, Kentucky. I know that from there, the train takes two more hours or so to get to Poncton, which is the stop closest to Mountain Hollow."

"Ah," said Charlie with a teasing twinkle in his eye. "Horseback riding, of course. Got to know how to ride a horse if you're going to be a fairy-tale princess."

Ruthie sighed inwardly. Charlie's needling, even the gentle joshing that it was, only made her all the more determined to prove herself. She was pleased when the conductor came past and spoke to her as if she were a grownup, saying, "Hello there, Miss Smithens. By your ticket, it looks as if you're going farther than usual today."

"Yes, sir," said Ruthie.

"Enjoy your trip," said the conductor.

"Thank you, sir," said Ruthie.

The train was stuffy and crowded full to overflowing with families traveling away from Cincinnati for holiday visits. Ruthie was so tense and excited that it seemed to her the minutes were dragging by even more slowly than the miles were chugging by. It seemed as if the train would *never* get to their stop! She couldn't concentrate on her book, even though she was in the middle of one of her favorite stories, "East of the Sun and West of the Moon." It was a nice distraction when she and Charlie got up and traded seats with an elderly man and woman who didn't like riding facing backwards.

Later, when Ruthie took out sandwiches for an early lunch for herself and Charlie, she gave some to two teenage girls across the aisle. As they ate, she chatted with them about where they were going.

There was a little boy in the seat behind them who was crying and fretful, so Ruthie, who remembered very well how it felt to be bored on a train, made a puppet out of her purple-flowered hankie and amused the boy so that his mother could rest.

"Thank you, Miss," said the boy's mother, smiling. "I'm on my way to a big party that my hometown has every year between Christmas and New Year's Day. It's at the church hall, and everyone in the whole town comes. There's food and music all day long, so I need to save my energy for dancing."

"It sounds wonderful!" said Ruthie.

Just then the conductor called out, "Next stop, Lewis Falls. Lewis Falls, next stop!"

"Poncton's after this," said Ruthie to Charlie, looking at the train schedule. "I wish I knew the best way to get from Poncton to Mountain Hollow."

"I don't know either," said Charlie. "Our family always drives when we visit Aunt Millie."

The elderly lady piped up. "Deary," she said to Ruthie, "did I hear you say that you are going to Mountain Hollow?"

"Yes, ma'am," said Ruthie. "We're getting off at Poncton."

"Well, you could do that," said the elderly man, turning to face Ruthie. "But if you're walking, it's faster if you get off at Lewis Falls. There's a logging road that runs right along the creek bed from Lewis Falls to Mountain Hollow. It's steep and unpaved, but it's much shorter."

Charlie looked doubtful. But Ruthie said, "Thanks! We'll get off at the next stop then."

But even Ruthie had her doubts when she and Charlie clambered down off the train at Lewis Falls. First of all, there wasn't really a station. There was just a rough wooden platform. Secondly, the only other passengers who got off the train at Lewis Falls were the two teenage girls she'd shared lunch with, and they disappeared down the hill right away. Worst of all, the logging road the old man had told them about was more like a muddy gully than a road. It wound up the mountain, zig-zagging under low-hanging tree branches that were all gnarled and twisted together. *Like the brambles that grew up around Sleeping Beauty's castle,* Ruthie said to herself. She knew better than to say it aloud to Charlie, who'd only scoff if she mentioned a fairy tale and who already thought she was goofy Ruthie, a less-than-reliable guide.

EAST OF THE SUN
AND WEST OF
THE MOON

As they began to trudge up the hill, Charlie asked, "Are you sure we were right to believe that old man on the train?"

"Well, of course!" said Ruthie. She acted more confident than she felt. "Though I do wish we didn't have to walk all the way."

Just then, Ruthie and Charlie heard a jingling sound behind them.

"Hey there!" said friendly voices. Ruthie's heart lifted to see the two teenage girls from the train. They were riding in a rickety old horse-drawn wagon, driven by a man who looked as if he must be their father. "Hop in!" said one of the girls. "Pa says we can give you a lift as far as Ferndale. The road splits there, and you can head off to Mountain Hollow."

"Thanks!" said Ruthie and Charlie with grateful grins.

There was far too much rattle and bang in the wagon for conversation, but the two girls and their father started to sing at the tops of their voices, so Ruthie and Charlie joined in:

Every morning, every evening,
Ain't we got fun?
Not much money, oh, but honey,
Ain't we got fun?
There's nothing surer: the rich get richer
    and the poor get poorer.
In the meantime, in between time,
Ain't we got fun?

They were bounced and jostled so much in the wagon that Ruthie felt as if her bones were being shaken apart, and the old horse plodded along more slowly than she and Charlie had stumbled along on foot. But the singing was cheering and riding was better than walking, which Ruthie and Charlie quickly appreciated after they were dropped off at

Ferndale. They set forth, huffing and puffing, up the branch of the road the girls had told them led to Mountain Hollow. The logging road was so slick and muddy that Ruthie slid back two steps for every step forward she took. The sky was a sullen gray overhead, and soon a stinging sleet began to fall. Ruthie knew that if she wasn't so hot and sweaty from walking, she'd be freezing.

"You know," said Charlie, "there wasn't any actual sign saying that this road leads to Mountain Hollow. We're just blindly trusting strangers again." He was quiet for a moment and then he went on. "I suppose you're thinking that this sort of thing happens all the time in fairy tales. You're kind to strangers, sharing food and things, and then it turns out that they help you get where you need to go. Even," he said with a smile, "if it's 'east of the sun and west of the moon.' But that doesn't work in real life, Ruthie."

Ruthie sighed. "I know you think I'm silly, Charlie," she said.

"Not silly so much as mistaken," said Charlie. "You think everyone is like you, nice and honest and wanting to help. But the world's not like that. People are going to take advantage of you. They're going to let you down. If you are foolishly optimistic, you're just going to be disappointed."

Ruthie slogged along, icy slush caked on her shoes and icy sleet trickling down her back. She knew that Charlie had had a terrible disappointment in his life. He had been supposed to go to college, but when the Depression came and Mr. Kittredge lost his job, there was no money to send him. So instead, Charlie was working, loading newspapers onto trucks before dawn every day. Ruthie understood that the world had let Charlie down.

Ruthie struggled to say what she had in her head. "I don't really believe that life always works out happily like fairy tales do," she said slowly, "and the wishes-come-true and the happy endings aren't the only reasons I like fairy tales. I like them because they show that no matter what happens to us, it's how we act along the way that matters. We still get to choose what kind of people we want to be. And, well, I guess I'd rather be foolish but hopeful about people than smart but stingy and distrustful."

Charlie looked at Ruthie out of the corner of his eye, as if he was considering what she had said.

Then, suddenly, his face lit up. "Hey!" he said. "I know where we are!" He pointed to a narrow path that went off to the left. "Aunt Millie's cabin is just up this path a ways," he said. "And Mountain Hollow is a mile or so past that." He grinned at Ruthie and gave her a congratulatory wallop on the back, saying, "I guess we've found 'east of the sun and west of the moon' after all."

The path to Aunt Millie's cabin was crisscrossed by little streams and pocked with puddles hidden under soggy leaves. Ruthie's shoes were so soaked, she didn't see how they could be any wetter. They squished with each step and water oozed out of them. But now that Ruthie and Charlie knew that they were almost there, they both felt so cheered up that they sped up and forgot all about being wet and cold. They walked even faster when, through the leafless trees, they saw the welcome sight of Aunt Millie's cabin ahead.

Kit had told Ruthie that Aunt Millie's cabin was next to the school where she taught. Ruthie was not

 surprised to see that the school
was shut up, dark and empty.
It was Christmas vacation, after
all. But she was surprised, heart-
sinkingly so, to see that Aunt
Millie's cabin also looked deserted. The door was
shut tight, and there was no movement from inside
and no sound except the dreary plink, plink, plink of
falling sleet.

Charlie knocked and called out, "Aunt Millie?"

But no one answered. It was plain to see that
Aunt Millie was not at home. *Oh no,* moaned Ruthie
silently. She'd thought that getting to Aunt Millie's
cabin would be the hard part of the trip. It had never
occurred to her that Aunt Millie would not be home.
Worries wormed their way into Ruthie's thoughts.
What if we can't find Aunt Millie? she wondered. *Our
whole trip will be wasted, the Kittredges won't get the
money they need, I'll confirm everyone's opinion that I'm
useless, and everything, everything will be lost.* Ruthie
shivered, as much from dread as from the cold.

Charlie was too polite to say, "Now what?"
But Ruthie could tell by the discouraged slump
of his shoulders that that's what he was thinking,

"Aunt Millie is probably visiting friends in town," said Ruthie.

and she did not blame him.

"Well!" she said. She put *her* shoulders back, remembering her resolution to prove her worth, and made her voice sound brisk and sure. "Aunt Millie is probably visiting friends in town. We'd better go see."

Without a word, Charlie followed Ruthie down the mountain toward the little town that was Mountain Hollow. With every step down, Ruthie fought to keep her hopes up. She wished with all her might, *Please let Aunt Millie be there. Please let us find her. We've got to.*

The sky over the mountains had lost all color and a soft, whispery snow had begun to fall when Ruthie and Charlie walked down the main street of Mountain Hollow. It was a tiny town. Ruthie saw that there was only one bank, one post office, one store, and a few little houses. The snow muffled the sound of Charlie and Ruthie's footsteps and seemed, in fact, to have silenced the whole town. It was as if the snow were some sort of magic sleeping dust that had put everyone to sleep. Every building looked as empty and deserted as Aunt Millie's cabin had.

"This place is a ghost town," whispered Charlie. "Where *is* everybody?"

"I wish I knew," said Ruthie.

"It's like an enchanted village out of one of your fairy stories," said Charlie. "Everyone vanishes between Christmas and New Year's Day."

Something stirred in Ruthie's brain. She remembered what the young mother on the train had said to her about the big party her hometown always had between Christmas and New Year's Day. Could it be that Mountain Hollow had a party, too?

Just then the answer floated toward Ruthie. As soft and as light as the snow in the air came the faint sound of music.

"Charlie," asked Ruthie, "where's the church?"

Charlie tilted his head to show the way. "It's just up ahead on Front Street," he said.

"Come on!" said Ruthie joyfully. She ran, bent forward into the snow. The closer she got to the church, the louder the music sounded, dancing out into the air to beckon her. Even more welcome was the heavenly aroma of wood smoke and food. When Charlie heard the music and smelled the food, he caught up with Ruthie, grabbed her hand, and pulled her along so fast, her feet didn't seem to touch the ground.

Charlie opened the door of the church and led Ruthie down the stairs to the church hall. As they entered the hall, Ruthie thought that no glittering ballroom in any fairy castle could ever have looked as beautiful as the room in front of her. Not that the room was fancy, not at all. It was as plain as a barn, with only a few pine boughs tucked behind the wall lights for decoration. But it was full of light and noise and people—young, old, medium, and even babies—having a rollicking good time. Long tables were laden with food. There were golden-brown turkeys, buttery biscuits, pink hams, orange mashed yams, pies that looked miles wide, and cakes many layers tall. The floor shook underfoot because of the dancers' feet and everyone else stomping along to the music. And best of all, the room was positively hot, which made it feel like paradise to Ruthie.

Suddenly, the room was quiet. Every face turned toward Ruthie and Charlie, who stood, beaming and dripping melted snowflakes, at the door.

"Hi, folks," said Charlie.

"Heavenly day!" said a bustling woman Ruthie knew at once must be Aunt Millie. "Charles Jackson Kittredge, is that you?"

"Yes, ma'am, Aunt Millie, it is," said Charlie. He put his arm around Ruthie's shoulder. "And this is Kit's friend Ruthie."

"You're welcome as sunshine, of course," said Aunt Millie as she hugged first Charlie and then Ruthie. "No one's sick or hurt at home, are they?"

"No, no," said Charlie.

"Well, then," said Aunt Millie in her peppery twang, "I've got to ask. What in tarnation are you two doing here?"

"That," said Charlie, with a sideways smile at Ruthie, "is a long story."

Aunt Millie propelled them toward a table. "In that case, sit down and have something to eat and drink," she said. "Your story will keep, but I've never seen two sorrier-looking creatures than the pair of you. You're like to fade if you don't get some food inside you right quick."

In the next few minutes Ruthie felt like Beauty in "Beauty and the Beast," because it seemed as if invisible hands whisked away her sodden coat, hat,

43

shoes, and socks to dry by the heat and gave her thick red socks and a toasty warm blanket to wrap up in while she waited. A steaming plate of the best-tasting food she'd ever eaten in her life appeared in front of her and, as if by magic, refilled itself— no matter how much she ate! A bunch of friendly girls just her age sat around Ruthie, chatting easily with her and making her feel comfortable and immediately at home. Ruthie had never met Aunt Millie, who was too busy being a teacher to come to Cincinnati, but it was impossible to feel shy around her, especially after Aunt Millie spotted Ruthie's book in her lunch basket.

"Are you reading 'East of the Sun and West of the Moon'?" Aunt Millie asked her.

"Yes," Ruthie admitted.

"One of my favorites!" stated Aunt Millie.

"Really?" asked Ruthie, surprised. She blurted out, "I've never met a grownup who reads fairy tales before."

"They have the wisdom of the ages in them," said Aunt Millie in her teacherly manner. "Folk tales, fairy tales, tall tales, myths, and legends have inspired some of the greatest literature ever written.

Even my own favorite author, William Shakespeare, based some of his finest works on legends. And he put fairies and magic and princesses in lots of his plays. Why, it would be a waste and a shame not to know the old stories!"

"And," laughed Charlie, "there's nothing Aunt Millie dislikes more than waste."

"Too true!" said Aunt Millie. "And I'm afraid time's a-wasting now." She drew Ruthie and Charlie aside to a quiet corner where they could talk privately and said, "So, as Shakespeare would say, 'tell me in one word.' What do you need?"

"Help," said Charlie. He explained to Aunt Millie about the money the family owed to the bank, and Ruthie explained how she had discovered that the Kittredges were going to be evicted December twenty-eighth if they couldn't come up with the money.

"Dad will be back from Florida with some money by January second," Charlie said, "but that will be too little and too late. So we're here to ask you for an emergency loan."

"The money's yours and welcome," said Aunt Millie.

Charlie hugged Aunt Millie. Then he said

solemnly, "I promise you we'll pay you back as soon as we can."

"Oh, I know you will," said Aunt Millie. "But don't let your dad fret about it. There's not much use for money in these parts anyway. We grow what we eat, and there's nothing much to buy. Besides, I've never noticed that money made a day much longer or me much smarter, so what's the use of it?" She stood up and gestured to a meek-looking little man. "Thurgood," she said, "let's go. I need to get my money out of the bank."

The meek man blinked. "But Miss Millie," he said, "it's after three o'clock. The bank is closed."

"Great day in the morning!" exclaimed Aunt Millie. She fixed the banker with a flinty glare. "Thurgood, you whippersnapper," she ordered, "open up that bank for me or I'll tell everyone how long it took you to learn your fractions when you were my student thirty years ago!"

Everyone laughed, even Thurgood.

CHAPTER

FOUR

—

WISHES COME TRUE

 "Now," said Aunt Millie crisply when she and Thurgood returned from the bank with the money, "Charlie and Ruthie, which one of you is going to take responsibility for bringing this money safely to Cincinnati?"

"I think Ruthie should," said Charlie, which surprised Ruthie and pleased her, too.

"Is that all right with you, Ruthie?" Aunt Millie asked.

"Yes, ma'am," said Ruthie, nodding. She stepped forward and opened her pocketbook.

Aunt Millie put the money into Ruthie's pocketbook, and Ruthie shut the clasp with a satisfying, secure *click*. She held on to the strap with both hands. Nothing would separate her or Charlie from this precious money.

Aunt Millie watched with approval. "Well, Ruthie," she said, "as Shakespeare says, 'Some are born great, some achieve greatness, and some have greatness thrust upon them.' You've just had quite a great responsibility thrust upon you, especially for such a young sprout. But you showed that you have stick-to-itiveness getting here. I'm sure it wasn't easy. So I think you've proven that you can be trusted."

"Thank you, Miss Millie," said Ruthie, glad to have impressed her. "I promise I'll get the money to Cincinnati."

Thurgood cleared his throat. "I hate to be the bearer of bad tidings," he said, "but I don't see how you're going to get back to Cincinnati tonight. You've missed the last train."

"What?" gasped Charlie, white in the face.

"No!" wailed Ruthie. "That can't be! We've got to get the money back to Cincinnati tonight. It has to be in the bank tomorrow or everything is ruined."

"Well, there is one more train that runs through to Cincinnati tonight," said Thurgood, "but it doesn't stop at Poncton *or* Lewis Falls."

"It will tonight!" said Aunt Millie forcefully, raising her fist in the air. "We'll flag it down. Come on! Step lively, now, everybody! We have a train to stop."

The church hall went topsy-turvy and got loud again as everyone bundled up in hats and coats. Ruthie scrambled to put her socks and shoes on, too, hopping on one foot and then the other, trying to keep up with the crowd. Outside, in the bracing cold, Ruthie saw that the snow had stopped, the sky was clear, and the last rays of the setting sun washed the world in a soft, pink glow. Around her, little children shrieked with delight and fell backwards into the snow just for the sheer pleasure of it. Every grownup in town who had a truck or a wagon filled it full of people, and every person carried an unlit lantern.

The next hour was the most exciting hour of Ruthie's whole life so far. She was scooped up and plunked high in the seat of a sleigh, and a heavy wool blanket was tucked around her legs. The sleigh did not look at all like the elegant silver sleigh that Kit and Ruthie had admired in the store window. It was made of rough wood that had once been painted red,

and it was pulled by two broad-backed, black horses.
The horses were so eager to run that they twitched
and quivered, making the bells on their harnesses
jingle merrily. Then, with truck horns
honking, wagon wheels clinking, horse
bells ringing, and everybody shouting,
the wild caravan careened down the
narrow road called the "haul road"
because loggers used it to haul trees off
the mountain. Ruthie memorized every detail of the
thrilling ride so that she could tell Kit how the frosty
night air smelled like Christmas trees and felt smooth
and cold on her face, how the blanket smelled like
horses and felt scratchy on her legs, and how the
sleigh swooshed so effortlessly over the snow that
it seemed to be sailing. *This is just how I imagined it
would be to ride in a sleigh like the sleigh that Kit and I
saw,* Ruthie thought, *only it's a million times better.*

When the sleigh and the trucks and wagons slid
into the Poncton train station, everyone jumped out.
They lined up in long lines on both sides of the train
tracks and, passing the flame along one to the other,
lit their lanterns. By now the sky was blue-black,
with only a slim sliver of a moon above surrounded
by thousands of tiny stars.

"Here she comes!" someone hollered.

All the people, young and old, tall and short, swung their lanterns so that light arced and swayed in the darkness. The people shouted out, too, and with a terrifying, ear-splitting *screech*, the huge black train screamed to a skidding halt. Sparks flew, and gusts of steam and smoke billowed out from the train as if it were a monstrous dragon breathing fire into the bitter cold night. Ruthie grinned. Even a ferocious dragon had to obey Aunt Millie's commands!

A conductor leaned out of the space between two cars. "What's going on?" he barked harshly.

51

"We're stopping your train, Earl," Aunt Millie answered calmly.

"Is that you, Miss Millie?" the conductor asked sheepishly.

"It is," said Aunt Millie. "We've got two passengers for you."

"Oh," said Earl weakly. "Well, then, all aboard."

After one last hug from Aunt Millie, Ruthie and Charlie climbed onto the train. Everyone called out, "Good-bye! Come back soon! Good luck, Ruthie and Charlie!" They swung their lanterns as they waved good-bye.

Ruthie ran to a window and waved back wildly. She watched until the train went around a curve and the last lantern disappeared, its light gone out, *poof!*, like a candle extinguished. Ruthie sank back into the seat as the train gathered speed. Even then, when she couldn't see anything but darkness outside the window, she was pretty sure she could still hear echoes of people cheering and calling out, "Good-bye! Come back soon! Good luck, Ruthie and Charlie!"

Ruthie certainly intended to be vigilant and to stay fully awake and alert every inch of the way home, holding on tight to her pocketbook with its hard-won contents. But it was warm on the train, and Ruthie was soon struggling to keep her eyes open.

"Hey, Sleeping Beauty," Charlie said kindly, "go ahead and snooze. Don't worry; I'll hold on to the pocketbook. You're losing your grip."

So, in spite of herself, Ruthie fell asleep and slept so soundly that Charlie had to shake her awake when the train pulled into Cincinnati. Ruthie rubbed her eyes. Her face was red and wrinkly because Charlie had rolled up his jacket and put it under her cheek for a pillow, her hat was askew, and her shoes were so streaked with mud that they'd never be the same again. Ruthie yawned. She stumbled tiredly along behind Charlie, who carried both the pocketbook and the empty lunch basket while they climbed the hill toward their homes.

When they got to the Smithenses' house, Charlie handed the basket and the pocketbook to Ruthie. "Here you go," he said. "You can give the money to your father, just as you and Kit planned." When

Ruthie hesitated, Charlie went on. "Would you like me to come inside with you and explain to your parents where you've been?" he asked.

"Uh, no thanks," said Ruthie, distracted. She was glad that it was dark out, because her face was a little bit flushed. It was harder than she had expected it would be to tell Charlie the new plan, the plan that would make possible her moment of triumph, when she changed everyone's opinion of her and showed that she was a hero. Ruthie took a deep breath and made herself speak up. "Charlie," she said, "I've been thinking. Wouldn't it be better if we gave the money to your mother right now and told her what we did—I mean, told her what happened? Then she could bring the money to the bank tomorrow."

"Okay," Charlie answered slowly. "If that's what you want."

Charlie turned to lead the way down the street to the Kittredges' house, but then he paused. "Before we do this, there's something I want to say," he said, "and it's thank you. Our family is lucky to have a friend like you, Ruthie."

Ruthie could not move or speak. For one split second she stood stock-still, the basket in one hand

and the pocketbook in the other. And in that split second, the whole wonderful, terrible, exhilarating, exhausting day flew through her head. She thought of all the people who had helped her so kindly, with such big-hearted, open-handed generosity and with never a thought of thanks. She thought of Aunt Millie, who had handed over the money without hesitation, purely out of love. She thought of Charlie, who'd been her partner in the adventure, following her despite his doubts, trusting her more and more as the day went on. How nice it was of Charlie to give her all the credit, how generous it was of him—and how *wrong*.

Ruthie felt as if she had been under a spell and Charlie's words about friendship had woken her up to a very simple truth: she had gotten the money because the Kittredges were her friends, not for praise and glory. Ruthie's sudden change of heart brought with it a change of plan. She no longer wanted to swoop in like the hero of a fairy tale and hand the money over and have everyone say, "Hurray for you, Ruthie! We are sorry that we underestimated you. You have saved us!" She did *not* want Mrs. Kittredge to thank her. In fact, Ruthie

55

squirmed at the thought of how disrespectful that would feel. Ruthie realized that the people whose opinions meant the most to her were Kit and Charlie. They knew the truth, and that was all that mattered.

Ruthie said, "I wish—"

"Uh-oh!" Charlie interrupted, grinning. He winced and raised his shoulders and both hands, pretending to protect himself. "I've heard you wish before," he said, "and I've learned today that your wishes have a way of coming true. What's your wish this time?"

"My wish," said Ruthie carefully, "is that you and Kit don't tell anyone that I had anything to do with getting this money." Ruthie looped the basket over her arm, opened her pocketbook, and gave the money to Charlie. "I think it would be better that way."

"Are you sure?" asked Charlie.

Ruthie was very serious. "I've never been more sure of anything in my life," she said wholeheartedly.

"Aunt Millie will tell my parents eventually," said Charlie as he put the money into his coat pocket.

"Well," said Ruthie, shrugging, "just keep me a secret until then, or as long as possible, anyway."

"Okay," said Charlie, smiling. "Your wish is my command."

Ruthie smiled, too, and started to go up the steps to her house. When she stood in the glow of the porch light, she turned back and said, "You know what, Charlie? Thanks for coming with me today. I'm glad you did. I'd do the whole thing over again."

From the dark, Ruthie heard Charlie laugh and then call out, "Me, too." Then he added, "Goofy Ruthie."

Somehow, there was something about the way he said it that made it sound like praise to Ruthie.

A week later, Kit, Ruthie, and Stirling were in Kit's backyard looking at trees. Looking when the leaves were down was the best time to see all the branches, and the three friends were trying to choose which tree they'd build a tree house in when they built a tree house.

"I guess we should say *if* we build a tree house," said Kit as they wandered inside to the kitchen

to warm up. "Because I sure don't know when, if ever, we'll be able to build it."

"I know you've wanted a tree house for a long time," said Ruthie kindly. "But don't give up. Sometimes wishes take a while to come true."

It was cheerful and crowded in the kitchen. Mr. Kittredge, who had returned from Florida the day before, was sitting at the kitchen table folding napkins and telling the boarders, Charlie, and Mrs. Kittredge about his trip. "Of course, the best part of the trip was coming home," Mr. Kittredge said. "Especially when I found out that we'd been saved from eviction just in the nick of time. Now *that* was a wish come true, thanks to Charlie here." Mr. Kittredge thumped Charlie proudly and lovingly on the back.

"Ruthie," said Charlie, "you are the expert on wishes. I'm wondering: can a person ask another person if he can override her wish? If you say yes, you'll make my wish come true."

"Mine, too!" Kit chimed in.

Everyone looked at Charlie and Kit as if they were crazy—everyone except Ruthie, that is, who smiled a tiny bit and gave Charlie a reluctant nod.

"Yes," Ruthie said.

"Good!" said Kit, smiling broadly at Ruthie.

"Yes, good!" said Charlie. "Because I want to tell a story. It's a true story about people we all like. In fact, the hero is Ruthie. Not the Ruthie we *thought* we knew, but really, truly Ruthie. My story has a happy ending, and like all wonderful adventures it begins, 'Once upon a time . . .'"

LOOKING BACK

APPLES AND KINDNESS: GETTING THROUGH THE GREAT DEPRESSION

*Empty storefronts, with signs announcing the closing
of business, were common during the Depression.*

The Great Depression affected everyone in America,
but not all families were affected in the same way. Kit's
family nearly lost everything after Mr. Kittredge lost
his business, but Ruthie and her family were lucky—
Ruthie's father did *not* lose his job. The Smithenses
could afford everything they needed, plus luxuries
such as the ballet tickets and lunch in a fancy restaurant
that Ruthie and Mrs. Smithens generously planned as
a Christmas gift for Kit and her mother. But as Ruthie
discovered, generosity can be tricky—and she had to
be very careful and respectful about trying to help Kit
without offending her pride.

As the Depression deepened and more people lost their jobs, money, and homes, sometimes the only thing they had left was their pride. Accepting help from friends or neighbors often was viewed as taking a handout—and taking handouts was *not* something that resourceful and independent Americans wanted to do.

That's why a group of girls in a small New Jersey town found a way to help others secretly. They formed a club called the Secret Helpers. Each girl paid dues of 10¢ a week, which they used to buy bread and soup. Then, once a week, they filled a box or a basket with the food they had bought, as well as shoes and clothes, and left it at the door of a family in need.

The Secret Helpers deliver a box of food.

Receiving the makings of a meal helped a family in need.

The new president, Franklin Roosevelt, and his advisors also understood that for Americans to preserve their dignity, they needed work, not just money to get by.

Americans let the government know that they wanted jobs, not handouts.

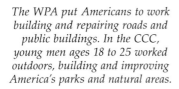

The WPA put Americans to work building and repairing roads and public buildings. In the CCC, young men ages 18 to 25 worked outdoors, building and improving America's parks and natural areas.

USA WORK PROGRAM WPA

The government programs they created, such as the Works Progress Administration (WPA) and the Civilian Conservation Corps (CCC), were designed to give Americans jobs, not handouts. People like Kit's Uncle Hendrick criticized these programs and called them charity, but most Americans were grateful for the work—and for the fact that the government was trying to solve the problems of the Depression.

Like the president, First Lady Eleanor Roosevelt also believed that Americans had to help themselves. Mrs. Roosevelt reached out to Americans by writing a weekly newspaper column called "My Day," which was printed in 180 newspapers nationwide. In her column, she wrote about the people she

Eleanor Roosevelt at her typewriter

met and the things she saw in Washingon, D.C., and about her extensive travels around the country.

The start of one of Mrs. Roosevelt's columns

Because of her column, many Americans felt that they had a friend in Eleanor Roosevelt. She received hundreds of thousands of letters from adults, teenagers, and even children. Some people wrote to ask for specific things, such as new shoes for their family, a dress to wear for graduation, or a piano, but many wrote asking for jobs. Like most Americans, they wanted a long-term solution to their problems, not a short-term fix. There was little that Mrs. Roosevelt could do for individuals, but she did reach out and listen carefully, making Americans feel heard.

As Ruthie and her mother figured out, sometimes the only thing that could be given—and accepted—was kindness. Other gifts, such as the apples that Ruthie brings to the Kittredges, had to be offered carefully and sensitively.

Friends arriving with everything needed for a surprise party

In some communities, neighbors held "surprise parties." They collected food, clothes, and toys—and sometimes even small amounts of money—and then knocked on a family's door to surprise them with a party. The caring and love were appreciated as much as the gifts that were delivered.

Throwing a "rent party" was another way for friends to help one another. When rent payments were due, a party would be organized and everyone who attended the party donated whatever they could afford.

Thanks to her teacher, this girl from the mountains of Virginia was able to complete high school.

Some people opened their homes. One Virginia schoolteacher made room for a bright, talented 13-year-old girl who was about to quit school to work and help support her family. Instead, the girl moved in with the teacher and helped out with household chores in exchange for her room and board while in high school.

Americans sometimes were surprised by how well they could adapt. One city girl and her family moved to a farm for the summer in order to save money. The girl worried that she'd be bored without

This city girl learned all about collecting eggs when she spent a summer on a farm.

her friends and without city things like movies. But by summer's end, she realized that she was sad to leave— she'd made new friends, had learned about both the hard work and the pleasures of farm life, and had come to appreciate the farm family that had so generously rented rooms to her city family. What had started as a hardship ended up being a wonderful experience.

Ruthie couldn't solve all of the Kittredges' money problems, but she *could* show Kit how important their friendship was, and that Kit's worth wasn't measured by how wealthy her family was. Ruthie gave Kit love, courage, self-respect, and hope—gifts that would last a lifetime.

A Sneak Peek at

Meet
Kit

*When the bad news of the Depression hits too close to home,
Kit worries about how her family's life will change.*

Kit pulled her article out of her big black typewriter and marched outside to sit on the steps and wait for Dad to come home. She brought her book about Robin Hood to read while she waited.

She had not been reading long before the screen door squeaked open and slammed shut behind her. Kit didn't even lift her eyes off the page.

Her older brother Charlie sat down next to her. "Hi," he said.

Kit didn't answer.

"What's eating you, Squirt?" Charlie asked.

"Nothing," said Kit as huffily as she could.

Charlie looked at the piece of paper next to Kit. "Is that one of your newspapers for Dad?" he asked.

"Yup," said Kit.

Charlie picked up Kit's newspaper and looked at the headline. "'It's Not Fair,'" he read aloud. Then he asked, "What's this all about?"

"It's about how it's wrong to blame people for things that are not their fault," said Kit. "For example, *me*, for the mess this afternoon."

"Aw, come on, Kit," said Charlie. "That's nothing. You shouldn't make such a big deal of it."

"What's this all about?" asked Charlie.

"That's easy for *you* to say!" she said.

Charlie took a deep breath in and then let it out. "Listen, Kit," he said, in a voice that was suddenly serious, "I wouldn't bother Dad with this newspaper today if I were you."

Kit slammed her book shut and looked sideways at Charlie. "And why not?" she asked.

Charlie glanced over his shoulder to be sure that no one except Kit would hear him. "You know how lots of people have lost their jobs because of the Depression, don't you?" he asked.

"Sure," said Kit. "Like Mr. Howard."

"Well," said Charlie, "yesterday Dad told Mother and me that he's closing down his car dealership and going out of business."

"*What?*" said Kit. She was horrified. "But . . ." she sputtered. "But *why?*"

"Why do you think?" said Charlie. "Because nobody has money to buy a car anymore. They haven't for a long time now."

"Well, how come Dad didn't say anything before this?" Kit asked.

"He didn't want us to worry," said Charlie. "And he kept hoping things would get better if he just hung on. He didn't even fire any of his salesmen. He used his own savings to keep paying their salaries."

"What's Dad going to do now?" asked Kit.

"I don't know," said Charlie. "He even has to give back his own car. He can't afford it anymore. I guess he'll look for another job, though that's pretty hopeless these days."

Kit was sure that Charlie was wrong. "Anyone can see that Dad's smart and hardworking!" she said. "And he has so many friends! People still remember him from when he was a baseball star in college. Plenty of people will be glad to hire him!"

Charlie shrugged. "There just aren't any jobs to be had. Why do you think people are going away?"

"Dad's not going to leave like Mr. Howard did!" said Kit, struck by that terrible thought. Then she was struck by another terrible thought. "We're not going to lose our house like the Howards, are we?"

"I don't know," said Charlie again.

Kit could hardly breathe.

"It'll be a struggle to keep it," said Charlie. "Dad told me that he and Mother don't own the house completely. They borrowed money from

the bank to buy it, and they have to pay the bank
back a little every month. It's called a mortgage.
If they don't have enough money to pay the
mortgage, the bank can take the house back."

"Well, the people at the bank won't just kick
us out onto the street, will they?" asked Kit.

"Yes," said Charlie. "That's exactly what
they'll do. You've seen those pictures in the
newspapers of whole families and all
their belongings out on the street
with nowhere to go."

"That is not going to happen
to us," said Kit fiercely. "It's *not*."

"I hope not," said Charlie.

"Listen," said Kit. "How come Dad told Mother
and *you* about losing his job, but not *me*?"

Charlie sighed a huge, sad sigh. "Dad told me,"
he said slowly, "because it means that I won't be
able to go to college."

"Oh, Charlie!" wailed Kit, full of sympathy
and misery. She knew that Charlie had been looking
forward to college so much! And now he couldn't
go. "That's terrible! That's awful! It's not *fair*."

Charlie grinned a cheerless grin and tapped

one finger on Kit's newspaper. "That's your headline, isn't it?" he said. "These days a lot of things happen that aren't fair. There's no one to blame, and there's nothing that can be done about it." Charlie's voice sounded tired, as if he'd grown old all of a sudden. "You better get used to it, Kit. Life's not like books. There's no bad guy, and sometimes there's no happily ever after, either."

At that moment, Kit felt an odd sensation. Things were happening so fast! It was as if a match had been struck inside her and a little flame was lit, burning like anger, flickering like fear. "Charlie," she asked. "What's going to happen to us?"

READ ALL OF KIT'S STORIES,
available at bookstores and *www.americangirl.com.*

MEET KIT • An American Girl
Kit Kittredge and her family get news that
turns their household upside down.

KIT LEARNS A LESSON • A School Story
It's Thanksgiving, and Kit learns a surprising
lesson about being thankful.

KIT'S SURPRISE • A Christmas Story
The Kittredges may lose their house.
Can Kit still find a way to make Christmas
merry and bright for her family?

HAPPY BIRTHDAY, KIT! • A Springtime Story
Kit loves Aunt Millie's thrifty ideas—until Aunt Millie
plans a pinch-penny party and invites Kit's whole class.

KIT SAVES THE DAY • A Summer Story
Kit's curiosity and longing for adventure
lead her to unexpected places—and into trouble!

CHANGES FOR KIT • A Winter Story
Kit writes a letter that brings changes and
new hope—in spite of the hard times.

◆

WELCOME TO KIT'S WORLD • 1934
American history is lavishly portrayed
with photographs, illustrations, and
excerpts from real girls' letters and diaries.